For my students, past and present, and for those who love kimchi and can't live without it.
— E. K.

Text & Illustrations by Erica Kim
The artist used colored paper, hanji, and digital art to create the illustrations for this book.
Hanji is a Korean traditional handmade paper made from the inner bark of the paper mulberry tree.
The cover was designed by Cha Consul and the book was designed by Elizabeth Jayasekera.
The production was supervised by Ceece Kelley.

ISBN 978-1-953859-27-3

Library of Congress Control Number: 2021951778

A partial image of the product packaging for Shin Ramyun, which appears in the illustration on p.21,
is used with the kind permission of Nongshim Communications USA.

First edition 2022. Printed and bound in China.

Distributed by Lerner Publishing Group, Inc.
241 First Avenue North
Minneapolis, MN 55401 U.S.A

For reading levels and more information, look for this title on www.lernerbooks.com

Soaring Kite Books, LLC
Washington, D.C.
United States of America
www.soaringkitebooks.com

KIMCHI, KIMCHI EVERY DAY

ERICA KIM

 Soaring Kite Books

I eat **KIMCHI** every day.

I like **KIMCHI** every way!

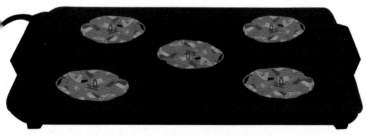

I like kimchi, all the kinds!

I like kimchi's

LITTLE LINES!

Kimchi Pancake,

ROUND
and CRUNCHY.

Kimchi Dumplings, **PINCHED** and **PLUMP,**

NIBBLE, NIBBLE,

eat them up!

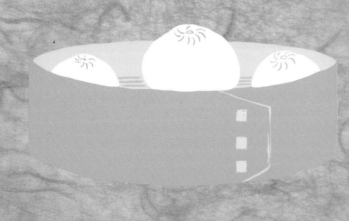

Kimchi Stew,

in a pot,

Kimchi Kimbap, in a roll,

OPEN WIDE
and eat it WHOLE!

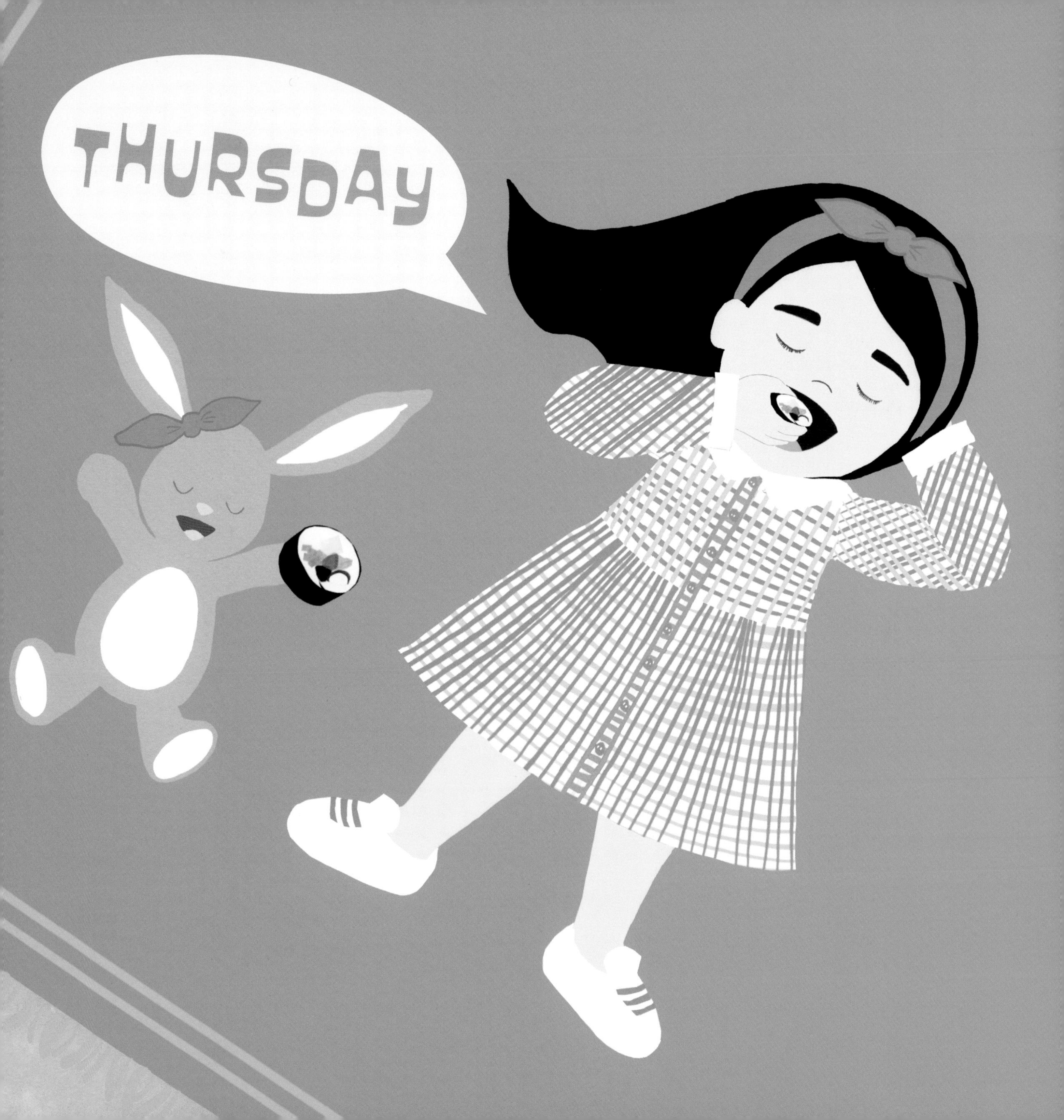
THURSDAY

KIMCHI FRIED RICE —

FRIDAY

it's the best!

CRACKLE, CRACKLE,

leaves a mess!

I eat **KIMCHI** every day.
I like **KIMCHI** every way!

Kimchi Glossary

Kimchi is a crunchy, salty, and spicy Korean dish made from pickled vegetables. It is seasoned with hot chili pepper flakes, garlic, green onion, ginger, and sometimes fish sauce.

There are hundreds of kinds of Kimchi! Kimchi can be made in bulk and shared with family, friends, and neighbors. It can be eaten alone as a side dish or used to create yummy dishes.

Kimchi Pancake
김치전
"Kimchi Jeon" —
beef or pork, kimchi,
and scallions mixed in
batter and pan-fried.

Kimchi Dumplings
김치만두
"Kimchi Mandu" —
beef or pork, kimchi,
vegetables, tofu, and
noodles pinched into a flour
wrapper then steamed,
boiled, or fried.

Kimchi Stew
김치찌개
"Kimchi Jjigae" —
beef or pork, kimchi, scallions, and tofu simmered into a hot stew.

Kimchi Seaweed Roll
김치김밥
"Kimchi Kimbap" —
meat, kimchi, rice, vegetables, and egg wrapped in a seaweed roll.

Kimchi Fried Rice
김치볶음밥
"Kimchi Bokkeumbap" –
meat, kimchi, rice, and
vegetables stir-fried
in a pan and topped
with a fried egg.

Ramyun
라면 –
instant noodles that are
often eaten with fresh
kimchi on the side.

Try it at home!

 On a hamburger or hot dog

 In tacos or quesadillas

 On top of fries or a baked potato

Kimchi Facts

- **Banchan 반찬 —** small side dishes served with any Korean meal. Kimchi is the most popular type of banchan.

- **Kimchi Refrigerator 김치 냉장고 —** a refrigerator that keeps kimchi at a special temperature to help the fermentation process, maintaining its freshness for months.

- **Ong-gi 옹기 —** a traditional clay pot that stores kimchi.

- **Gimjang 김장 —** the making of large amounts of kimchi, typically in November and early December.

- **National Kimchi Day 김치의 날 —** celebrated on November 22nd, with many kimchi festivals taking place on this day.

- **Kimchi Museums 김치 박물관 —** there are several museums dedicated to kimchi, such as Museum Kimchikan in Seoul, Korea.

Erica Kim

Erica Kim is an author, illustrator, and elementary school teacher. She has an M.A. in Early Childhood Education from Teachers College, Columbia University. Erica loves everything about working with young students, from being able to cultivate a love of learning to the often funny and heart-warming moments that arise each day.

She grew up in Connecticut but also spent several formative years living in Seoul, Korea. She now lives in Virginia and enjoys working with cut paper and incorporates this material into her illustrations.

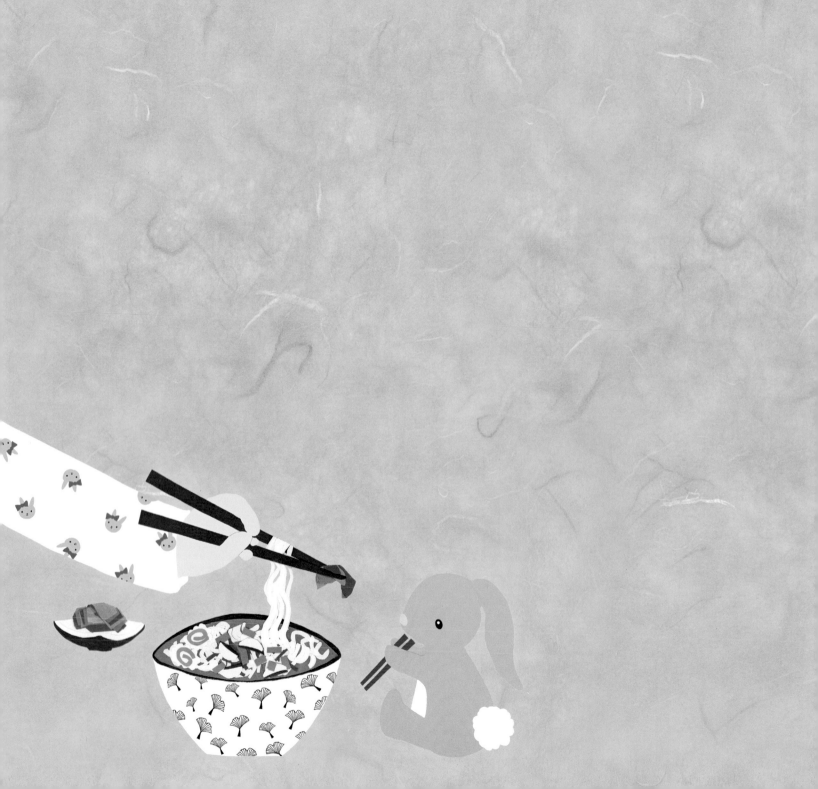